5 Lesbians Eating a Quiche

Evan Linder and
Andrew Hobgood

With contributions by Sarah Gitenstein,
Mary Hollis Inboden, Meg Johns, Thea
Lux, Beth Stelling, and Maari Suorsa

A Samuel French Acting Edition

SAMUELFRENCH.COM
SAMUELFRENCH-LONDON.CO.UK

ISBN 978-0-573-70116-0

www.SamuelFrench.com
www.SamuelFrench-London.co.uk

For Production Enquiries

United States and Canada
Info@SamuelFrench.com
1-866-598-8449

United Kingdom and Europe
Theatre@SamuelFrench-London.co.uk
020-7255-4302

Each title is subject to availability from Samuel French, depending upon country of performance. Please be aware that *5 LESBIANS EATING A QUICHE* may not be licensed by Samuel French in your territory. Professional and amateur producers should contact the nearest Samuel French office or licensing partner to verify availability.

5 LESBIANS EATING A QUICHE was first produced by The New Colony in Chicago, IL (Andrew Hobgood, Artistic Director; Evan Linder, Artistic Director) on June 24, 2011. The production was directed by Sarah Gitenstein and assistant directed by Jaime Totti, with sets by Nick Sieben, costumes by Nathan Rohrer, lighting by Garvin Jellison, sound design by Gary Tiedemann, props design by Shelby Wilson, and special effects by Ruth McCormack. The Script Supervisor was Joel Kim Booster. The Production Stage Managers were Jessica Whitington and Stephanie Shum. The cast was as follows:

LULIE STANWYCK .... Mary Hollis Inboden
WREN ROBIN .... Meg Johns
GINNY CADBURY .... Thea Lux
DALE PRIST .... Maari Suorsa
VERONICA "VERN" SCHULTZ .... Beth Stelling

5 LESBIANS EATING A QUICHE received its New York City premiere on August 10, 2012 as part of the New York International Fringe Festival, a production of The Present Company (Elena K. Holy, Producing Artistic Director) at the Living Theatre. The production transferred to the SoHo Playhouse (Darren Lee Cole, Artistic Director) on September 21, 2012 as part of the FringeNYC Encore Series, and began an extension on October 16, 2012, presented by John Arthur Pinckard, as part of the SoHo Playhouse's 2012-2013 Season. The production was directed by Sarah Gitenstein, with set and special effects by Kevin McClintock, costumes by Nathan Rohrer, lighting by Nicholas J Carroll, sound design by Gary Tiedemann, and props design by Shelby Wilson. The Associate Producers were Jaime Totti and Noah Lemaich and the Production Stage Manager was Smyra Yawn. The cast was as follows:

LULIE STANWYCK .... Rachel Farmer
WREN ROBIN .... Meg Johns
GINNY CADBURY .... Caitlin Chuckta
DALE PRIST .... Maari Suorsa
VERONICA "VERN" SCHULTZ .... Thea Lux

The full-length version of *5 Lesbians Eating a Quiche* was commissioned by The New Colony and based on a ten-minute version, written and directed by Evan Linder, presented in 2010 by Collaboraction at Sketchbook X in Chicago, Illinois.

The playwrights would like to give special thanks to: John Arthur Pinckard, Anthony Moseley at Collaboraction, Nicholle Dombrowski and Charlie Bills at the Dank Haus, Elena K. Holy and Britt Lafield at the New York International Fringe Festival

CHARACTERS

LULIE STANWYCK – President

WREN ROBIN EVENTS – Chairwoman

GINNY CADBURY – Secretary

DALE PRIST – Historian

VERONICA "VERN" SCHULTZ – Buildings and Grounds Chairman

SETTING

A community center in middle America where the annual Quiche Breakfast of the Susan B Anthony Society for the Sisters of Gertrude Stein is being held.

TIME

Today, 1956

PRODUCTION NOTES

Any lines that are book-ended with brackets can be said by the actor however they feel each night, but the substitution should keep to the written line's intent. Wren's [I can't! I can't! Oh, this is dangerous.] could become [Oh, ladies! I can't! It's too much.] The purpose of these brackets is to inject spontaneous moments into each performance that will never be seen the same way twice. The actors should follow their instincts and say how the character is thinking/feeling in the moment. If, in that moment, nothing new comes to mind – you can always adhere to what is written.

When you come upon a "/" in the script, it means that the following line should begin at the slash mark and the line being spoken should continue to the end of the sentence.

Each time the name of the sisterhood is spoken, the rest of the characters should join in on "...Society for the Sisters of Gertrude Stein."

The melody for the song in Scenes I and V should be improvised.

PLAYWRIGHTS' NOTES

As a satire on the melodramatic fears of America during the Cold War and Today, there will be a temptation to play *5 Lesbians Eating a Quiche* as a campy comment on society, complete with knowing winks to the audience. Avoid this trap at all costs! The script, when delivered simply and with honest emotion, will take care of the satire on its own. The actors need not think on how to make the script funny. Instead, they should focus on how to make the women real. These five women do not in any way find the events of the play funny. In fact the complete opposite is true: this is the most serious day of their entire lives. While it is easy for the outside world to look at fundamentalists and see their beliefs and traditions as absurd and outrageous, fundamentalists themselves see only the absolute truth and majesty of their mission. They are never commenting on the absurdity of the situation.

These women never speak in double entendres. The fact that their literal words read as such to the audience goes unnoticed by the women. All of the comedy in this play originates from one source: honest, real people delivering ridiculous dialogue and tackling insane situations as if what they are saying and doing is commonplace and expected by the audience. For every ounce of honesty you inject into *5 Lesbians*, the laughs will be returned by the pound, and the deeper the audience will slip into seeing themselves as your Fellow Widows.

Perhaps most important: Always remember that these women love each other. Lulie even loves Ginny despite the hazing Lulie imposes on her as their newest officer. They are not only fellow officers but best friends. The audience should know this the moment they burst into the room.

All audience members should receive a name tag when they enter the space. The names should all be popular women's names before 1950. Any time you see an audience member being referenced by name in the script – you should call them by the name on their name tag.

Each performance will feature a male audience member who is pre-selected (without their knowing it) to play Marjorie throughout the show. He should receive a "Marjorie" name tag and be seated in the audience where he is most visible to the other audience members. No one loves Marjorie.

Now let the Breakfast Begin!

– Evan Linder & Andrew Hobgood

Scene I

*(***WREN***,* **DALE***, and* **VERN** *all come bursting out into the crowd. They are friends with everyone. They ad lib their hellos with the audience: "LUCILLE! [a member of the audience] How're your orchids doing?!"* **WREN** *becomes overwhelmed by it all and has to hoot off a little steam. She then brings the meeting to order.)*

WREN. Oh, Vern! Oh my!! OH! This looks beautiful!

(She can't stop herself from hooting.)

O O O O O O O O O O O O O O O O H ! ! ! ! OOOOOOOOOOOOOOOOOOH!!!!

(She composes herself. Or at least makes a great effort.)

WREN. Ladiiiiies!

(The sisters gather. She addresses the audience.)

Fellow Widows! Ladysisters! Welcome! Welcome to the [INSERT TODAY'S DATE] meeting of the Susan B. Anthony Society for the Sisters of Gertrude Stein! I am your Events Chairwoman, Wren Robin, and I am so happy to welcome you all to the 1956 Quiche Breakfast!

(The widows applaud.)

VERN. Hop to it, Dale! That's a photo.

*(***DALE*** leaps out to snap a photo of* **WREN** *which* **WREN** *is immediately ready for. Click.* **VERN** *is pacing around the audience, inspecting the troops.)*

DALE. Nice pose, Wren!

*(***WREN*** melts.)*

WREN. Thank you Dale. Isn't Dale just lovely this morning? I know most of you probably walked in and thought to yourselves, "Who is this…beautiful, porcelain doll?!" But it was just Dale!

(Remembers suddenly!)

WREN. *(cont.)* Oh! And let us all give a round of applause to Vern Schultz for our Community Center's fully – modernized facelift! Doesn't this place look just beautiful!

VERN. Thank you, Sisters!

*(**GINNY** rushes in.)*

GINNY. Sisters! Lulie is almost done judging the quiches and then we'll be ready to start the meeting.

WREN. Oh, sisters! Did you hear that?

*(**WREN** and **DALE** busy themselves setting up.)*

VERN. Ginny. I waited for you earlier. I thought we were going to walk over together.

GINNY. Oh Vern, I completely forgot! I've been so frazzled getting ready for today.

VERN. No. It's fine. Louise walked over here with me after I fitted her for a pant suit.

*(**VERN** gives a seductive smile to the audience member. **GINNY** gives Louise a look.)*

GINNY. I didn't even know you and LOUISE were friends.

VERN. *(trying to make her jealous)* Well, she's not my first choice. But I could certainly get used to her kind of walk.

GINNY. No! Vern, truly I've just been pre-occupied. I haven't been able to think about anything but quiche!

VERN. You're excited about eating that prize quiche, are you?

GINNY. More than anything!

VERN. Very well. I'll accept that.

WREN. Ginny, how many quiches were submitted this year?

GINNY. Well, we have [NUMBER OF AUDIENCE MEMBERS ATTENDING] sisters here in attendance today, and all but one submitted a quiche.

DALE. Who wouldn't submit a quiche?

*(**VERN** has spotted someone in the audience.)*

VERN. Looks like there's someone here who's too ashamed to let the light of day see her quiche ever again.

(She walks up to the audience member that has been pre-selected as Marjorie.)

VERN. Isn't that right, Marjorie?

(The sisters gasp.)

WREN. *(trying to be polite)* Oh my. Marjorie. I didn't see you. Out there with all the other widows.

DALE. Yeah, Marjorie. We're used to seeing you up here with the other officers.

GINNY. *(She remembers the stories.)* Oh…Marjorie.

VERN. That's right. The Marjorie.

WREN. Now, now, sisters. We can all discuss Marjorie's fall from grace immediately after the meeting.

VERN. Let's do that by the way. Immediately after the meeting. Let's get that on the agenda. Ginny!

*(**GINNY** pulls out a small notepad.)*

GINNY. I have made note of it as an Action Item.

DALE. [Oh! An action item!]

WREN. Oh sisters! The anticipation is so incredible!

GINNY. I'm so excited for my first quiche breakfast!

WREN. Yes! And welcome to you Ginny! We're all so fortunate to be together like this today. Not that I have to tell you that. This is such an important day to all of us, of course.

VERN. Amen sister!

WREN. It makes you appreciate how brave our dear founder, Lady Ulrika Monmont was. To live alone in the woods all those years, amongst the creatures and birds and berries...until the day when she came across that colony of chickens. The chickens who would produce the backbone of this sisterhood.

WREN. The egg!

GINNY. The egg!

DALE. Oh! That reminds me...I have a surprise for everyone.

*(**DALE** mischievously smiles and heads towards the exit.)*

GINNY. Now now Dale, you must hurry. Lulie is almost ready.

DALE. I'll be really quick!

*(She hands her camera to **GINNY**.)*

If anyone strikes anything resembling a pose –

GINNY. Absolutely. I won't let you down.

*(**DALE** goes to the exit but quickly turns around in a "pose", testing **GINNY**. **GINNY** is immediately ready for it and clicks.)*

GINNY. You were testing me...

DALE. I was testing you.

GINNY. *(with pride)* You were testing me!

DALE. Guilty!

*(**DALE** exits.)*

WREN. Ginny, I have a new agenda that I'd like to add to the agenda for today!

GINNY. The agenda is almost / filled, Wren.

WREN. Thank you! This is important! While I was walking here this morning – it struck me: we need more public spaces to share! We have a park. And it's beautiful. But we need more! So I would like to propose –

– for the very first time –

– that we build and then donate a ranger station!

VERN. Wren, we've been over this. There's no use for a Ranger Station. Because there are no rangers in this town.

WREN. Oh, I don't think that's truuuue! I think that if we build the station, the rangers will come to it! And it could be right in the center of town. I know the perfect place for it! Right in the center! And if there is ever an emergency, I'll just pull out the ol' phone tree, call everyone up and say, "Yoodle-oo! Meet me at the Rangers Station!" and you all would know what I was talking about! Oh, and I could keep an eye out for any kind of Soviet invasion –

VERN. Whoa, whoa, whoa. In the event of a Communist attack – there's a much safer place to go than a Ranger Station.

WREN. Where are you suggesting?

VERN. Well, Wren. I'm suggesting you're standing in it.

WREN. In what?

VERN. Only the safest place in America Today. You see, Wren, as buildings and grounds chairman, this facility is under the care of my person, which means, by extension, you are all under my person, and while anyone is under my person...Ginny!

GINNY. Yes?

VERN. I expect to be obeyed.

GINNY. *(trying to not succumb to this...)* I've...made note of it.

VERN. Give 'em the tour, Ginny.

GINNY. Well I did have this later on the agenda, but I suppose we can break from procedure for this one matter.

VERN. That's right.

GINNY. [Widows, as you probably know when Vern –]

VERN. Ginny.

(She leans in a bit.)

Like I asked you to do it.

GINNY. [Vern, I feel silly –]

VERN. *(the final word)* Ginny.

(**GINNY** *stands at attention like she is reading a Royal Proclamation.)*

GINNY. *(in a VERY British accent)* Upon the impeachment of the previous Buildings and Grounds Chairman… Marjorie –

(They turn and glare once more.)

One Veronica Schultz was elected to the post and tasked with renovating this Community Center. Under her direction, this facility was outfitted with a top-of-the-line security system.

VERN. *(stepping over to the security door)* Exhibit A. As you know, a point of contention between myself and the beautification committee was this security door. Though eventually we were all able to see eye to eye.

GINNY. If anyone needs to step outside to the powder room during the breakfast, you are more than welcome to do so.

VERN. *(to Marjorie)* Respectfully.

(**VERN** *should hold this look as long as the audience allows. And the other sisters agree with it. This is serious. The last time Marjorie used the bathroom…let's just say it was disastrous.)*

GINNY. Yes. Now, in the event of an atomic bomb, there are –

(**DALE** *re-enters with a large framed portrait. The audience can only see the back of the frame.)*

DALE. Look what I have!

VERN. *(to* **GINNY***)* That's okay. We can cover that part later.

WREN. Oh my! What is that Dale?

DALE. I thought Lulie would love this! I was digging through the archives the other day and made the most incredible discovery!

(She turns the portrait around so that everyone can see. An absolutely hideous picture of Lady Monmont holding an axe is revealed. Ooohs and Aaahs.)

DALE. I found this old candid – very candid – portrait of Lady Monmont, taken when she was clearing the subdivision now known as "Oak Tree Falls."

(Murmurs of agreement from the widows.)

DALE. Now you can see here she is returning from the Colony of Chickens. I deduced this from the specially designed egg satchel she is carrying. And just then...a mighty oak, fell before her, and landed right in her path. And this portrait was taken just as she began to chop that tree into pieces and clear her path. And even though this was candid, I look at this and think, "But that's a pose."

*(**WREN** is caught by such surprise that she hoots a little.)*

DALE. Exactly! A tree lands, she sees it, and she's dealing with it. She has to build a town, she's got a lot of eggs, she's got a tree in her way, but she's dealing with it. And it's the sheer drama in this pose. She was just one of those women...a woman who knew how to pose. Even when she wasn't.

*(**DALE** has discreetly landed in a pose which a caught off guard **GINNY** scrambles to click a photo of.)*

WREN. Oh, Dale. That was beautiful! Lulie will be so touched.

WREN. Look at her. Sisters! None of us would be here if it weren't for her. Her determination became our future.

*(She gives the portrait back to **DALE** who goes to hang it.)*

VERN. Hey Dale, I thought I saw you bring two big portraits into the meeting today.

DALE. Keen set of peepers, ya got there Vern. The other one is in the kitchen. I'll be revealing that one at the end of today's quiche breakfast. It's an even bigger surprise than this one!

WREN. *(reprimanding)* Dale Prist! Too many surprises!

(She starts to crack a smile.)

WREN. *(cont.)* No such thing! Oh, the anticipation! Could this breakfast be any more exciting?

(Suddenly, we hear a handbell being run offstage. The widows get all excited.)

GINNY. [Everyone sit up! Do you want Lulie to have a conniption?!]

*(**VERN** goes to dim the lights. The Quiche Breakfast is about to begin!)*

*(The sisters all line up. **GINNY** takes out a pitch pipe out of a tiny pouch attached to her dress and tries to give the sisters their note. She doesn't quite hit the note. Hurriedly puts the pitch pipe back in the pouch.)*

GINNY. [We know what a "C" sounds like.]

*(They all agree with **GINNY**. They begin to sing. At the start of **LULIE**'s solo, she makes her grand entrance holding a covered silver dish with this year's Prize Quiche in one hand and an envelope in the other.)*

ALL.

WE ARE THE SUSAN B. ANTHONY SOCIETY
FOR THE SISTERS OF GERTRUDE STEIN
WE ARE A STRONG AND VIB-A-RENT SOCIETY
TOGETHER TIL THE END OF ALL TIME

LULIE.

AND YOU KNOW WE STAND AS ONE,
OH MY, IS THAT QUICHE DONE?

ALL.

(I THINK IT'S DONE!)
WE ARE ONCE, TWICE, THREE TIMES THE LADY
WHEN WE'RE STANDING ARM IN ARM

WREN/GINNY.	**DALE/VERN.**
LINKED AS ONE	(LINKED AS ONE)
HAND IN HAND	(HAND IN HAND)
WE ARE STRONGER	(WE ARE STRONGER)
THAN ANY MAN	(THAN ANY MAN)

ALL.

WE ARE ONCE, TWICE, THREE TIMES THE LADY WHEN WE'RE STANDING ARM IN ARM

LULIE. Well isn't that lovely. The female voice in unison. Even if we weren't singing about quiches, it would still send chills down my spine.

(This speech ends in an elaborate pose.)

WREN. Keep on your toes Dale! That's a photo!

LULIE. Where do I look?

*(**DALE** snaps **LULIE**.)*

DALE. Gorgeous as/always, Lulie.

LULIE. *(to the officers)* Hello fellow Widows!

ALL. Hello sister!

LULIE. *(to the audience)* Hello fellow widows!

*(The audience responds. But not up to **LULIE**'s standards.)*

LULIE. *(addressing the "Current Members" in the audience and the officers)* Sisters, let's give them our customary welcome. When we say, "Hello fellow widows!" I want to hear you shout a the top of your lungs, "Hello Sister!" Now let me hear it with pride! HELLO! FELLOW. WIDOWS!!

(They officers and the audience all cheer their response.)

LULIE. *(charged up by the response from the room)* Can you believe it is that time of year again? The tasting of the first quiche! I don't think I need to re-iterate the importance of the EGG to me and my life. All of our lives. As I explained in the forward of my best-selling textbook "Women Can Yes: the History of the Egg", the egg is as close to the Lord Jesus as a piece of food can get. So pure, so perfectly shaped, so delicious. I remember the first time I ate quiche.

(The widows sigh, thinking about their first times.)

I was so young. Sprightly. Naive. And that first bite. I didn't think I'd ever find others who enjoyed quiche as much as I did. And then I found you all. My sisters. My fellow widows. And I for one cannot wait for you all to try this year's Prize Quiche.

(The widows excitedly hubbub and gather around the table. **LULIE** *goes over to the portrait of Lady Monmont.)*

LULIE. Now, now, sisters! Who is responsible for this?

(beat)

DALE. I am, Lulie. I found it in the archives.

(beat)

LULIE. That's the most beautiful thing I've ever seen. Let us take a moment to reflect on how our founder suffered for our sake. Feasting off of nothing but bits of bark and moss. Working tirelessly to build a haven we now call home. This very day, all those years ago, was an historic day. She had promised herself that she wouldn't stop until her mission was complete. A modern day Noah! But she was exhausted and hungry. Sure that she couldn't possibly go on. Until she stumbled upon this very spot – the home of hundreds of wild chickens. Nests overflowing with a bounty of eggs. And from those eggs she drew the strength necessary to complete this town. I like to think Lady Monmont is looking down on us today and smiling. Oh, and she's eating a quiche.

(The sisters beam looking up towards Lady Monmont in Heaven.)

LULIE. Wren, as the Events Chairwoman, it is your privilege to honor our great hero by presenting this year's Prize Quiche.

GINNY. I wonder who's quiche we are eating first / this year?

LULIE. THIS year, I chose a very special quiche to begin the festivities. One of such beauty and imagination that I think it may be one of our best quiches ever.

GINNY. I can't take it! I just can't!

LULIE. She just "kaant". Isn't that adorable. This year, our first quiche shall be...

*(**WREN** reads the back of the envelope.)*

WREN. [Spinach. Red Onion. Gruyere. Rosemary. Asparagus.] Made with love by...

(She opens the envelope and reads the card:)

WREN. Veronica Schultz!

*(The widows squeal and congratulate **VERN**.)*

VERN. Stop it you guys.

(The sisters continue applauding.)

VERN. Stop.

(The sisters continue.)

VERN. Stop it! I'm serious. Stop.

GINNY. Lulie, if no one else has asked yet, may I do the unveiling of the quiche?

LULIE. Oh Ginny. Sweetheart, you must learn to stop being such an attention hog. You're in America now! Vern can unveil her own quiche.

VERN. Hey Ginny. We can do it together. Come here.

WREN. Oh, isn't that lovely! Sisterhood in action.

*(**GINNY** and **VERN** place their hands on the dish. They unveil the quiche. They almost lose it, but still try to maintain decorum. They all lean down and take a big whiff. Whoa, that smells good. **LULIE** shows the quiche to the audience and encourages an "Ooh! Aah!" response. Finally:)*

DALE. The suspense is killing me! Take a bite Lulie!

LULIE. Now now Dale. It would be rude of me as the president to take the first bite. [Therefore I will go immediately to my left – and then one more over.]

*(Poor **GINNY** gets passed over.)*

LULIE. Ginny, it's just Wren's year to get to try first.

GINNY. Yes.

LULIE. Chin up sweet girl. Maybe next year. Maybe not.

(**WREN** *holds the fork to her heart. Enraptured, this bracketed moment goes on for quite a long time.)*

WREN. [I can't! Oh, I can't! Thank you! Oooooh. I can't!]

GINNY. [I will if / you don't want to…]

WREN. I'm going to do it Ginny!

*(***WREN** *continues with ooh's, oh's and ah's as she digs the fork into the quiche and selects the perfect bite. She lifts it up, smiles as* **DALE** *takes a photo, and just as she's about to:)*

WREN. [I can't! I can't! Oh, this is dangerous.]

*(***WREN** *finally takes a bite. The sisters cannot move. How is it? Finally* **WREN** *looks at the other sisters in horror and covers her mouth. The other officers do the same. Oh no!* **WREN** *finally uncovers her mouth revealing a huge satisfied smile.)*

WREN. It's tooo good!

LULIE. Oh, thank Jesus.

WREN. This might make everyone here just lose their senses!

VERN. That's what I was going for.

LULIE. Wren, I take it the quiche has passed the test?

WREN. Well, if Vern's quiche has anything to say about it, 1956 is going to be our best year yet!

GINNY. Oh Vern! I knew you could do it!

LULIE. Surely, its considerably better than what Marjorie submitted last year.

VERN. Yeah, tomato and mushroom. That was a real winner Marge.

DALE. Ew. I can't even think about it. She might as well have just put meat in the quiche.

LULIE. Dale Prist! Wash out that mouth! We do not even joke about putting meat in a quiche.

DALE. Sorry, Lulie.

LULIE. Need I remind you all of this sisterhood's golden rule?

ALL. No men. No meat. All manners.

LULIE. Thank you.

(beat)

Meat in a quiche! Can you imagine?

WREN. Remember Petunia Bradley?

LULIE. Remember her? I expelled her!

GINNY. Who's Petunia Bradley?

LULIE. This was before your time here Ginny. It was one of the darkest days the Susan B. Anthony Society for the Sisters of Gertrude Stein has ever seen. Four years ago, Petunia Bradley marches in here with a sausage quiche!

VERN. I can't even think about it.

LULIE. She marches in here, puts it down on the table, and tells us that we need to open our minds.

DALE. Ew.

LULIE. Broaden our horizons!

WREN. I'm going to be sick.

LULIE. I mean, can you imagine? Putting a sausage in a quiche. The moment you put meat in a quiche, it's all you can taste. It takes away from the cornerstone of what makes a quiche magical...

LULIE & GINNY. The Egg!

LULIE. *(annoyed with* **GINNY***)* THE EGG!

VERN. Yer darn tootin'.

WREN. Next thing you know, Lulie takes Petunia by the hair in one hand, takes that sausage quiche in the other hand, tosses them both right out the door.

VERN I daydream about that a lot. I just replay it in my head, over and over again. And I will. Laugh.

GINNY. *(catching a whiff of the quiche)* Sisters! We can't wait any longer!

(beat)

GINNY. *(cont.)* It just seems unfair…to keep the others waiting in hungry anticipation.

LULIE. Ginny.

(She holds the tension. And then:)

You are quite right. We can't torture our fellow sisters like this any longer. Let the breakfast begin! Wren, bring in the other quiches!

(Lights. Sirens. This is it. The Big One.)

Scene II

VERN. Ladies, here we go.

GINNY. What's going on?

WREN. Lulie, is there a drill today?

LULIE. *(keeping it presidential…)* Not that I'm aware of. We have to treat this as if its the real thing, ladies! To your posts!

GINNY. What do I do?

LULIE. The quiche, Ginny! For pete's sake! Protect the quiche!

DALE. Do you think it's the Commies?

LULIE. I wouldn't put it past them, Dale.

GINNY. Oh, God!

LULIE. But if they do bomb us, I'm sure we'll hit 'em back even harder.

VERN. Stop it! You're scaring her. / It's probably just a drill Ginny.

WREN. Are all of the sisters accounted for?

DALE. I'm going to check the powder rooms.

*(**DALE** exits.)*

GINNY. My cat. Rachel. She must be scared out of her wits.

(She turns to the security door nervously.)

GINNY. She's never been through a drill before. I'm just going to pop over and see how she's doing.

*(She moves towards the door. **VERN** sees her.)*

VERN. Ginny! NO!

*(She lunges to the door and lands between it and **GINNY**.)*

GINNY. Vern, I'll just be a moment –

VERN. Didn't you hear what Lulie said? We're treating this like it's the real thing. Do you realize what would happen to you if a bomb did drop?

GINNY. Yes, but –

VERN. Everyone and everything out there would be obliterated. And even if you could go out and get her, we couldn't let you back in. Even if we wanted to. You know that just as well as I do.

WREN. So we would all just die in here?

VERN. No one here has to worry about dying! I've been preparing for this ever since I replaced Marjorie.

LULIE. *(to Marjorie)* And you said she wouldn't last a week. You owe me ten dollars, Marjorie!

(suddenly disgusted looking at Marjorie's feet)

You know what? Just keep it and buy yourself some new shoes!

VERN. NO ONE. Is to go through this door unless I tell you to.

(turning to **GINNY***)* Understand?

(to the sisters) If Ginny had stepped out that door after an explosion, it would have sensed external radiation, and sealed itself shut. I've rigged the door so it can be opened once. Just ONCE in an emergency. But after that, the only way to re-open the door is with a welding torch. And that, I left under my bed.

LULIE. What about the window there?

VERN. You mean my quadruple-paned government engineered window? Did that myself. And the window treatments.

(The widows compliment **VERN***'s window treatments as* **DALE** *walks back in. The sirens and flashing lights abruptly stop. Everyone freezes. Waiting for the blast. After a few moments, the five officers slowly move together in the center of the room. They speak softly.)*

DALE. It's stopped.

WREN. Surely that's a good sign.

LULIE. Sisters, on a day as important as this, I think Uncle Sam will forgive us for continuing on with the meeting.

(They start to breathe easy again.)

WREN. There are worse things than dying at a Quiche Breakfast, after all.

(HUGE explosion. Flash of light from the window. It's happened.)

Scene III

(The sisters scream and duck wherever they can. **GINNY** *is the first to stand again.)*

GINNY. [Oh my God...I almost died.]

(She starts to have an anxiety attack.)

GINNY. [Oh my GOD!!!]

VERN. Ginny –

GINNY. [I would have been almost...halfway home!...if you hadn't stopped me...VERN!]

VERN. [Shhhhh. Ginny –]

GINNY. [RACHEL! She must be...I should be...dead right now!]

VERN. [No, Ginny!]

GINNY. I should have died. I should have DIED!

(As **VERN** *is walking* **GINNY** *back to the other officers,* **GINNY** *catches a glimpse of Marjorie sitting there, alive and well.* **VERN** *has to restrain* **GINNY** *from attacking "Marjorie".)*

GINNY. [YOU should have died! YOU SHOULD HAVE DIED, MARJORIE!]

VERN. Ginny, no! You were meant to live.

LULIE. She's right, dear. You were meant to SURVIVE! Like the rest of us.

WREN. That's right! Sisters! We should be thankful for Vern's preparedness. Because of her, we are alive!

GINNY. Yes. I suppose you're right.

WREN. And personally, I think that if I am to survive something like this, I can't imagine anyone better to survive it with. My sisters.

LULIE. That's the ticket Wren! Let's all be thankful that we are going through this together. Holding onto our dearest friends. And might I just say fellow widows, I'm so very proud of how everyone is taking this news. End of the world and all.

DALE. So what do we do now?

LULIE. Vern, why don't you tell the sisters about the provisions you've made for us here and then we can continue with the meeting! No need to let this spoil the day.

VERN. Sure thing Lulie. Now, we won't be able to safely emerge from here for another four years. Good thing, I have enough dried food back there to last all [NUMBER OF AUDIENCE MEMBERS ATTENDING, MINUS ONE] of the sisters here for exactly 208 weeks. If we ration properly, we should just make it.

GINNY. Um...actually, if I may. We have [CORRECT NUMBER OF AUDIENCE MEMBERS ATTENDING] here at the meeting today.

LULIE. Right. So someone needs to be killed.

GINNY. What?

LULIE. At some point.

GINNY. What are you saying?

LULIE. Soon.

GINNY. Is no one hearing this?

DALE. Ginny, Lulie's the president. She's our decision-maker. Don't be such a dip.

VERN. We aren't gonna kill anyone important. It will probably be somebody –

(She motions her head towards Marjorie. The lesbians consider this.)

GINNY. I guess that's not so bad...But four years! That's an awful long time to be together.

VERN. Nooo! It'll be great. It'll be like college.

GINNY. Well yes. Except without the men of course.

(The other ladies all look at each other. Smiles begin to creep. Maybe this isn't a bad thing?)

GINNY. Or Rachel. My cat. She would have been sitting right by my front door waiting for me to come home. She's probably just a puddle of whiskers by now.

*(**VERN** consoles her.)*

DALE. And my father. I didn't get to...say goodbye.

WREN. Dale, I've never heard you even speak of your father.

DALE. We had a really big falling out when I was three. But I was almost ready to forgive him. I was this close.

WREN. What did he do?

DALE. Well, it was 1932 –

LULIE. We don't need to get into that now, Dale. We've been through quite enough already. We don't need to start boring the sisters with our childhood traumas. My only loved one out there in that whole mess is my dear mother. But ever since her hands fell prey to that hand condition –

(She motions the condition with her hands.)

ALL. [Oh yeah. – That's right, her condition. –]

(They all demonstrate the condition with their hands. No version looks quite the same.)

LULIE. She hasn't really been of much use. It's a shame really. But none of that matters if we are not strong enough to first address the real tragedy that has befallen us today. Right outside that door is a table full of all those glorious homemade quiches, that we will never ever taste.

WREN. Oh no!

GINNY. My quiche!

LULIE. But do not fret. No, no, Vern has secured us some chicken coops in our food storage.

VERN. You bet I did.

LULIE. And, on my orders, filled those coops with 14 healthy, sturdy chickens to accommodate the egg-needs of this sisterhood!

(long beat)

VERN. That...I forgot to do.

LULIE. Vern, we've been through quite enough today. This is no time for jokes.

VERN. No, I'm serious. I totally forgot the chickens.

*(**VERN** begins to break down.)*

VERN. [It's been a really long week. Just a lot on my mind. Oh ladies, I'm so sorry. This isn't like me. I blew it! Oh man, I blew it big.]

DALE. *(cutting off **VERN**)* Oh, Vern. How could you.

LULIE. I knew you never loved quiche as much as I did –

VERN. Hey now, that's below the belt!

*(**LULIE** starts to lunge at **VERN** when **WREN** quickly steps between them and holds **LULIE** back.)*

WREN. Widows, we can't turn on each other! We must stay calm!

LULIE. But with no chickens in here for the next four years –

GINNY. There'll be no more eggs!

DALE. No more eggs means...

LULIE. Please don't. Don't say it!

WREN. *(suddenly realizing)* OH! No more quiche!

GINNY. *(Her stomach drops.)* No more quiche.

(beat)

VERN. I'm so sorry, Lulie. You know how much quiche meant to me.

(beat)

DALE. So this is the last quiche ever?

(long beat)

*(**WREN** steps forward first.)*

LULIE. No ma'am.

*(**WREN** quickly steps back to where she was standing. She smiles to prove that everything is okay. **LULIE** quickly moves to the table.)*

(The others join her. The five surround the quiche and treat it with reverence. It is holy and sacred. **LULIE** *slowly, one by one, begins to pass out the forks to the officers. She skips over* **GINNY** *and tosses the last fork onto the table.* **LULIE** *notices she is getting the "evil eye" from "Marjorie".)*

LULIE. What, Marjorie? WHAT!? We can't let it go to waste! Surely all the other sisters here understand that there is simply not enough quiche to go around for everyone.

VERN. They understand. It's getting cold. Let's do this.

(The lesbians all slowly, delicately dig in and take a bite together. Oohs, aahs and mmms. WHOAS! They ad lib as they mourn this last moment of ecstasy.)

WREN. [It's even better than the first bite!]

VERN. [I did a really good job.]

(The lesbians quicken the pace, beginning to fight over the quiche. **LULIE, DALE, WREN** *and* **VERN** *grab handfuls, devouring it ravenously and pushing* **GINNY** *out from the table. Determined to get her share,* **GINNY** *dives back into the feeding frenzy, mounts the table, digs her face into the quiche dish, and sensually devours the rest of it. The ladies all take a step back from the table so they can take this in. They become intrigued, then aroused. After a long, long while…)*

VERN. That is great technique.

WREN. Ginny…I had no idea…

LULIE. Ginny – it's the last one ever. Savor it, / darling girl.

DALE. DO NOT distract her. Look at that. She's doing it just right.

GINNY. *(finally coming up for air)* Oh no. I don't know what came over me. Truly, I don't.

(beginning to inch off stage)

[I'm so sorry. That was bad. Very, very bad. I'm so humiliated…]

DALE. Nothing to apologize about sister.

WREN. I should say not!

VERN. Ginny, sweetheart. Come here.

*(**VERN** moves in close. Very close.)*

VERN. You've got a little – just right there – little egg still on your face there.

(The sisters are nearly paralyzed as they watch what is about to happen. They look on, frozen with anticipation and repressed excitement.)

GINNY. *(Reaching up to get it)* Dearie me, how embarrassing.

VERN. No, no. I got it.

GINNY. Yes, but I can –

VERN. *(seductively pulling **GINNY**'s hand away from her mouth)* No. Ginny? No. I got this.

*(**VERN** slowly moves in for the kiss. **GINNY** starts to resist but is under **VERN**'s spell. **VERN** gets even closer.)*

VERN. That's right. Just let it happen.

*(They kiss, passionately. It's beautiful and lasts much longer than a kiss between friends. **LULIE** tries to speak. Finally:)*

LULIE. Sisters! No! We are still officers of this society!

*(**GINNY** breaks away, shocked.)*

VERN. *(picking a bit of egg off her lip)* Got it!

GINNY. [That was…Wrong. Very very wrong. I'm not – I'm not a…]

WREN. *(huge, sudden realization)* Widows! Don't you see? We don't have to pretend anymore. We needn't hide! We're the last ones left! It's just us! I say we use this opportunity to finally be honest with each other. And ourselves. We don't need to say "widows" anymore! We aren't widows!

(She steps forward bravely.)

[I've never been married!]

VERN. [Me either!]

DALE. [Me either.]

*(**WREN** is moved and inspired. She is overcome by the moment.)*

WREN. Oh sisters! I've wanted to say this for so long –

LULIE. Wren, watch yourself!

GINNY. Wren, no dear! Not in front of everyone like this!

LULIE. Sisters, this is getting out of hand! Order!

WREN. I gotta! I gotta say it! (sung)I gotta sing it out louuuuud! I am –

DALE. I'm a lesbian!

*(She stands in shock at what she has just done. The room is silent and all eyes are on her. She carefully walks over to **WREN** who is still processing what she just heard. **DALE** looks **WREN** in the eyes.)*

DALE. I'm a lesbian.

*(**WREN** nods.)*

And I can't even tell you how good that felt. And no one else is going to feel this wonderful feeling until you just say it.

(beat)

So if anyone else would like to say what I just said a moment ago...then I suggest you just do it. Anyone?

(beat)

Wren? Would you say it?

WREN. Of course I will, Dale. It would have sounded a lot better at the end of that powerful speech I was just making. But yes I'll say it, because it's true!

*(**WREN** gets herself back to the level she was at the end of her speech with a few hoots.)*

I. Am. A LESBIAN! And Dale gave me this bracelet!

(She holds her hand high so that everyone can see the charm dangling from it.)

DALE. And I gave me one too!

(She holds up her arm next to **WREN***'s showing her matching bracelet.)*

GINNY. Is everyone a lesbian?! Secret lesbian societies! This is exactly what I was warned about before I left Manchester. "Watch out for those Americans and their secret lesbian societies, they'll snatch you up!"

VERN. Snatch –

LULIE. May I remind everyone that there is still a meeting of the Susan B. Anthony Society for the Sisters of Gertrude Stein taking place!

WREN. Things have changed Lulie! We all better get used to it! Vern, it's so wonderful. You must! Say it now! We're the leaders here. None of the other sisters will have the courage unless the officers do it first!

GINNY. But Vern, you're not! Don't you see? This is peer pressure of the worst kind! You're not a lesbian! [You're just an unmarried 30 year old lady who enjoys a game of softball every now and again.] Please. Deep in your heart, you must know that this isn't right. We're ladies. We must act like it.

VERN. She's right sisters. You're right, Ginny. We must. Act like ladies. I think I may have given everyone the wrong idea earlier. I apologize. I'm not a...you know. I'm not. I just really, really enjoy quiche.

GINNY. Me too.

LULIE. Me too.

DALE. Me too.

WREN. Me too.

(beat)

VERN. I'm just joking. I'm a big old lesbian!

*(***WREN, VERN** *and* **DALE** *all celebrate together.)*

LULIE. Vern, I can't believe you! And in front of all the sisters?

VERN. Oh please Lulie, you don't think they're all lesbians?

(finding 2 men in audience)

VERN. *(cont.)* [I know CECILIA is a lesbian, I saw her push a lawnmower once! And DONNA owns riding boots and a saddle – but no horse!]

WREN. [PATRICIA over here is definitely a lesbian. She whittles her own toothpicks!] Come on PATRICIA! Say it! Say, "I'm a lesbian!"

(They all encourage the audience member to say it. When they do, the lesbians cheer loudly and encourage the rest of the audience to cheer.)

DALE. [And I've seen JUDY bake her own bread…In a KILN!] Are you a lesbian JUDY?!

(Again, they encourage the audience member to say it. There is much rejoicing as more and more sisters come out.)

WREN. [We've all seen the ball peen hammer ROBERTA keeps in her purse! Haven't we girls?!]

DALE. [What about LORRAINE! She brushes her hair with a hairbrush…made out of her own hair!]

WREN. *(to the whole audience)* Well you've all just gotta say it Sisters! Everyone together! WHAT ARE YOU?!

(They cheer at the audience members' response.)

VERN. And MARY BETH is either a lesbian or she's got a real funny way of thanking me for fixing her toaster.

DALE. Ginny, look! We're your sisters! No more secrets! You're one of us and you know it.

WREN. Of course she is!

LULIE. NO, SHE IS NOT!

(This stops the room. **GINNY** *is caught in the middle. 3 on one side of her,* **LULIE** *on the other.)*

LULIE. Ginny, if we are the only officers left with any sense of decorum, then so be it. Come here, sweet girl.

(**GINNY** *starts to walk towards* **LULIE** *and is stopped by…)*

VERN. Hey Ginny?

GINNY. Yes?

VERN. Ginny, remember the first time I fitted you for a pantsuit?

GINNY. No I do not, Vern.

VERN. Remember when I went to measure your inseam? And you let out that little noise?

GINNY. Not at all.

VERN. And I asked you what the noise was?

GINNY. [It was a…chair scoot]

VERN. And you said it was nothing.

GINNY. [A kitten…in the wind.]

VERN. And I asked if you had coughed, and you said…no. And then I asked if you'd maybe let out a really weird sneeze? And you said…

GINNY. No.

VERN. And then I said…

GINNY. "Well if it wasn't a cough and it wasn't a sneeze, then what was it, Ginny?

VERN. And you said…

GINNY. I don't know Vern, just keep measuring that inseam.

(A smile starts to creep across **GINNY***'s face.)*

Oh my, I am a lesbian.

DALE. YES!

(The widows cheer and applaud.)

LULIE. Ginny, no!

VERN. That's my girl!

LULIE. This is chaos! I won't stand for it! Order! Order!

VERN. How can you deny something so basic? We don't have to hide! In four years, do you think anyone out there is going to care if we're lesbians or not? There'll be so few people left that it won't matter anymore. It'll be 1960! We could probably all get married if we wanted to.

LULIE. Well, I never –

LESBIANS. [Come on Lulie. Come on girl. Come on out. You'll feel much better when you come out. Come on out now.]

LULIE. I'm –

GINNY. [It does feel quite good, Lulie. Go on. You can do it.]

LULIE. I'm…I'm pregnant.

Scene IV

(A long silence hangs over the room. Until:)

WREN. With a baby?

LULIE. Yes! Pregnant! I am with child.

GINNY. Well, Lulie!

(blows up her cheeks as if she's going to say something but just lets the air out)

Um…Congratulations! This…

VERN. Makes absolutely no sense whatsoever.

LULIE. I understand it must be a shock.

DALE. But…how? How did it happen?

(small beat)

LULIE. I fell on a turkey baster.

(small beat)

WREN. Well, I fall on turkey basters all the time, but they never have SEMEN in them!

LULIE. I'm not going to go into the sordid details right now. But if we're all being honest with each other I feel like you must know. I'm three months along. In six months, the Susan B. Anthony Society for the Sisters of Gertrude Stein is gonna have it's first child.

GINNY. You all must admit, it is a little exciting.

DALE. No it is not!

VERN. A baby? We're gonna have a baby?

*(**WREN** is suddenly awestruck by a thought. She gasps. The lesbians all look to her.)*

WREN. What if it's a boy…

(The sisters look at each other in shock. This is unprecedented.)

LULIE. Then we must prepare ourselves for that. To be perfectly honest, there's a good chance it is a boy.

GINNY. To be even more perfectly honest, the chances are still just 50/50. There's really no way for us to know what's coming outta there.

LULIE. Thank you, English Scientist.

(beat)

LULIE. Widows, I have another confession to make. And it's shameful.

WREN. Too many surprises! I'm still not over your last confession. We'll be down here for four years, can't we just spread out our secrets a little bit better? [Maybe save this next one for Christmas?]

LULIE. No more secrets Wren! You said it yourself. I know this baby is a boy, because I've...been craving meat.

DALE. Oh Lulie!

VERN. THIS IS WHY WE HAVE RULES!

WREN. A boy. What are we going to do with a boy? OH! Lulie. You could have a little penis inside of you right this moment!

(This absolutely mortifies **LULIE.***)*

GINNY. Oh, Wren stop it!

WREN. And it's just growing bigger and bigger every single day!

DALE. Ew.

LULIE. I've got to sit down.

GINNY. Dale! Fetch her some water!

DALE. Why me?

*(***DALE** *hurries off for water.* **GINNY** *goes to comfort her.)*

GINNY. You poor dear. We're all here for you, I promise.

VERN. Lulie. It wasn't really a turkey baster was it?

LULIE. Well –

VERN. So who's the father?

LULIE. Well, if you must know, his name is Pope Jones.

WREN. *(disgusted)* Oh, Lulie.

LULIE. No, no Wren. Not my cousin Pope Jones. There's another one.

WREN. Ohh.

LULIE. He lives two towns over.

VERN. Were we just not enough? Is that it? What in the world do you want with a child?

LULIE. Because God gave me eggs, Vern! Eggs! I knew God wanted me to hatch one! I needed to hatch! So as disgusting as the proposition was to me – and believe you me, Pope Jones was one disgusting proposition – I knew I was doing God's work.

*(**DALE** re-enters with water for **LULIE**.)*

DALE. *(curtly)* Here you are.

LULIE. Thank you, Dale.

GINNY. But don't you all see? Widows –

WREN. Lesbians!

GINNY. Lesbians! If we're the only ones left, we will be responsible for repopulating America. This baby is a blessing! We're going to need him!

VERN. You're right!

LULIE. *(slowly realizing)* Yes. Yes! This baby is going to save womankind! Once he's old enough, we'll need to start impregnating one of our members pronto!

*(**LULIE** begins to survey the audience, looking for the mother of her baby's baby.)*

GINNY. We're going to save America!

VERN. We're going to have a baby!

DALE. And that baby's gonna make one of us have a baby?

WREN. Yes, Dale, that's how it works!

(to the Sisterhood)

Well, we'll really need our youngest members to start preparing for that.

GINNY. *(checking her notebook)* Let's see here. Our youngest members...well, the youngest of all the lesbians here is – oh dear, it's Marjorie.

LULIE. NEXT!

GINNY. Next. Yes, the next youngest would be...Dale.

WREN. Oh my! I certainly have my misgivings, but you'd be the most beautiful mother I can imagine, that's for sure.

LULIE. Yes! I think Dale would be just lovely.

GINNY. What do you say Dale?

DALE. I'm not sure I could do that.

LULIE. The fate of the world rests atop your loins, Dale. What about that do you not understand?

DALE. No, YOU don't understand Lulie. I can have nothing to do with that child if its a boy. I haven't spoken to a man since I was three years old.

(beat)

VERN. How's that even possible?

DALE. I became quite good at it. I would ignore all the boys at school. I would cross to the other side of the street if I ever saw one coming. When I go to the deli, I just write down on a little sheet of paper "a half pound of potato salad, please" and just slide it across the counter. Keep my head down. No eye contact.

WREN. So you've never even spoken to a man –

DALE. Since I was three years old. That's right. Ever since my father...

GINNY. Oh sweetie, what happened?

DALE. I can't.

WREN. No more secrets. Remember?

DALE. I just can't –

VERN. Come on Da –

DALE. It was 1932.

(**DALE** *has crossed downstage and is looking out in the distance. A spotlight falls on her.)*

My parents had – *(squinting)* Oh my, what is that?

VERN. Oh, those are just the emergency lights I installed. They'll do that from time to time. I'm sure they'll shut off in a minute.

DALE. Sure. My parents had taken me and my sister to the lake for the weekend. My mother had bought me my first swimsuit, and I knew that when we got there, I would be able to swim. Oh, how I wanted to swim in that lake. I told my older sister Edith, "when we wake up tomorrow, I'm gonna go down to that lake, and I'm gonna swim." And Edith said "Oh, sweet little Dale. We're ladies. We can't exert ourselves by swimming. Do what I do. Just sit in the inner tube and float. Ladies float." But oh, I wanted to swim.

When I woke the next morning, my mother told me that Edith was already down at the lake with her inner tube. So my father took me down the winding path, and we look out in the distance and see Edith, all by herself, Just floating. Like a lady.

I ran down to the edge of the water. This was it. My first time to swim. I took my first tentative step into the water. Now until that point, the only time I had ever put my foot in water was when my mother would draw me a lovely warm bath. But this lake was cold. And to my three-year-old little foot, it was as if I had placed it in a lake of...sharp icy daggers.

VERN. Great imagery.

DALE. I screamed. I turned back and ran to my father crying. "Oh daddy! It's so cold. I can't!" My father just glared back at me. When he heard me say "I can't," he heard weakness. My father hated weakness.

And he raised up his hand, and said –"

*(**DALE** suddenly, almost demonically, becomes her father.)*

"You git in that warter, Deele! You git in that warter! You know you like it."

I cried uncontrollably.

DALE. *(cont.)* "DEEELE! You git in that warter. You know you like it." Edith leapt from her inner tube and tried swimming to shore to come to my rescue. She knew daddy had a temper. But she couldn't swim. She only knew how to float.

She was a lady.

My father screamed after her. "Edith! Swim, darling, swim!"

"Daddy! You have to go and help her!"

"Deele, I can't git in the warter! You KNOW I've got aquagenic pruritis!"

Now, I'm proud to say that I was advanced for a three year old. But I didn't know what aquagenic pruritis was. I still don't. But I knew it was something serious. My father started screaming at the top of his lungs.

"Get in that warter Deele! You know you like it! Save your sister!"

He continued screaming at me, as we both watched my sweet sweet Edith, sink like a stone in that lake. Never to be seen again.

(beat)

Until later that day when some fishermen pulled up her bloated body.

My father thought they were too rough when they were pulling her up and put one of the fishermen into a coma during a fit of rage. He was sentenced to ten years in prison. My mother was admitted to an asylum. And I just changed my name and moved on. Never spoke to a man again.

(The emergency lights turn off.)

GINNY. *(dabbing her eyes)* Oh Dale!

VERN. Come here, baby Dale. Auntie Vern's got a hug for ya right here.

*(**DALE** runs to **VERN** and weeps in her arms. All of the other widows go over to comfort her.)*

WREN. Oh, my lovely Dale.

DALE. Yeah, it was a tough break.

VERN. We know it was.

DALE. A real, sloppy tear.

LULIE. Oh sweetpea. We had no idea!

DALE. Thanks lesbians. I could have saved her though!

GINNY. Hush, now! You were so young! You did all you could!

WREN. You know we'll never let anything happen to you, don't you?

VERN. You know you're everyone's favorite, right?

WREN. Everyone says so.

ALL. *(to the audience)* [Isn't that right? Tell her!]

(The lesbians encourage the audience to let **DALE** *know how much they love her.* **DALE** *smiles and nods her thanks.)*

LULIE. Dale, we will find someone else. You will never have to speak to a man again. Not even this little bastard in here.

DALE. No! I have to move past all this. If the re-population of the universe rests on my shoulders, then I will do it!

LULIE. You don't have to Dale.

DALE. Yes I do! For Edith, and for the galaxy. Lulie, I will have your baby's baby.

LULIE. Deal, Dale.

(They shake hands. The lesbians celebrate.)

GINNY. I'm sorry you never got a chance to forgive your father Dale.

DALE. Me too.

WREN. And you never saw him again?

DALE. Nope. Not since his sentencing. I was there when they took him out in handcuffs and led him away.

GINNY. Must have been dreadful!

DALE. Yes. Especially for a three year old. I can still hear that judge's voice in my head. "You are a disgrace to your town! I sentence you to ten years in prison! May God have mercy on your soul Pope Jones."

(The other widows stop in their tracks. Horror!)

DALE. It was really scary.

WREN. Um, Lulie? Your cousin didn't go to prison ever did he?

LULIE. No. My cousin Pope is only 22 years old.

VERN. *(going behind* **DALE** *and pulling her hair back)* Did Pope Jones from two towns over look at all like THIS?

LULIE. AHHHH! Oh, sweet Jesus, that's him.

DALE. What? What's going on?

LULIE. Ginny, who's the next youngest after Dale?

GINNY. Um…me.

LULIE. Then Ginny, the job is yours! Welcome to motherhood.

DALE. But why?

LULIE. Dale! This is your brother!

DALE. *(Wait for it…NOW she gets it)* Oh!!

(As if she has been given a huge gift on Christmas morning, kneels down and speaks to **LULIE***'s belly.)*

Hey there, you little bastard. It's your big sis Dale. How ya doing in there? Do you think he can hear me?

LULIE. Don't matter none, Dale. You stay down there as long as you like.

DALE. We're all waiting for ya out here, buddy. You've got a roomful of lesbians ready to welcome you into the world. And one of them is going to have sex with you.

GINNY. *(nervously leaning down to the belly)* That would be me. Hellooo.

DALE. *(still to* **LULIE***'s belly)* I'm really glad I'm going to get to be someone's sister again.

VERN. Oh man, lesbians! We're gonna make it through this. I know it.

WREN. Yes, we've really gotta hand it to all of our fellow lesbians here today. No one lost their cool or ran for the doors. It's those calm heads out there that remind me why we break quiche every year and celebrate the strength of the egg that inspired the Susan B. Anthony Society for the Sisters of Gertrude Stein.

LULIE. Oh lord.

GINNY. Lulie, what is the matter?

LULIE. I hadn't thought of it like that...

WREN. What?

LULIE. What will become of him; growing up in a world without quiche? What kind of a mother will I be in a quicheless world? What if he can't taste it in my milk and he rejects my teat? What if he inherits momma's hand condition? A child without any access to the EGG for the first years of his life is more likely to grow up weak and frail.

VERN. Lulie, I said I was sorry about the chickens.

LULIE. I'm not laying blame, Vern. I'm just worried. Like a mother worries. We can survive off of these rations as grown ladies. But what about a growing baby boy? Without the vital nutrients that the EGG provides, will he just shrivel up like a little white raisin?

DALE. Vern! Do we have a freezer back there in storage?

VERN. You bet your sweet bippy we do.

DALE. Then we're set! We've still got all those quiches right outside this door. If we freeze them and ration them, then the little bastard's got some EGG.

VERN. Alright, hold on! Dale – the radiation levels out there would melt Velveeta in seconds. Nobody can withstand that level of radiation –

DALE. For how long?

VERN. Sixty, sixty-three sec – There's no way to tell.

DALE. There are two things you need to know about me:

*(**DALE** begins to take her dress off until she's down to her slip.)*

DALE. One: I was an all-star sprinter in high school. And two: I've never been sick a day in my life. I can do this!

(She starts towards the door. **WREN** *stops her.)*

WREN. Dale, I really…really appreciate what you're doing right now – but what are you saying, dear?

DALE. Words! I want to do this. I want to do for that little bastard what I was never able to do for Edith.

LULIE. I appreciate what you're trying to do –

GINNY. Dale. It's too dangerous.

DALE. Have you all forgotten the spirit of our great founder? In the words of Lady Monmont, "Deal with it!" And I'm going to. We've got those quiches, we've got a hungry baby, an atomic explosion…but I'm dealing with it.

(The sisters look at one another and confer silently.)

VERN. Alright. Let's do it. Here's the plan: Lulie, you hold the door. Ginny and Wren, get ready to grab the quiches. Dale – I'm watching the clock. At 45 seconds – I'm making you come back in whether you like it or not. Deal, Dale?

DALE. Deal.

VERN. Alright ladies! Let's make this happen! To your positions!

*(***DALE** *starts for the door.* **WREN** *is waiting there for her. Just as* **DALE** *is about to open the door, she grabs* **WREN**, *dips her, and kisses her. She yanks* **WREN** *back up, and in an instant she's out the door.* **LULIE** *holds it open. It looks heroic.)*

(The sisters wait anxiously and ad lib their worries: "Come on **DALE**" *"How much time does she have?" etc.)*

*(***DALE** *suddenly arrives back at the door with an armful of quiches. She hands them off to* **LULIE**. *At the sight of these glorious quiches,* **LULIE** *turns and hoists them*

high – the sisters go berzerk. But they don't see **DALE** *go running out the door again. The doors start to close.* **VERN** *sees it.)*

VERN. THE DOOR!!!

(The sisters scream. **WREN** *leaps for the door but misses it. She stands pressed against the door as she hears it seal itself shut.)*

GINNY. Vern! Do something!

VERN. I can't! The door sensed radiation. It's sealed.

LULIE. No!

VERN. Permanently.

WREN. Dale!

Scene V

(The ladies all cry, hold on to each other, console each other.)

GINNY. Why? Why??

VERN. She missed the safety instructions. I was gonna go over them with her one on one. I just – I – OH GOD!

LULIE. DAAAALE!!!!

GINNY. How much time does she have?

(beat)

VERN. She's not coming back.

(The four are speechless.)

WREN. Oh, my sweet, sweet Dale…

(The ladies softly cry together. Suddenly there is a tap at the window. **DALE** *is standing outside, her hands full of quiches.)*

DALE. Hey lesbians! I've got em! Open the door!

(The women stare in shock.)

VERN. Who's gonna tell her?

LULIE. Wren. You tell her.

*(***WREN*** nods. She gently approaches* **DALE***.)*

WREN. Dale…Dale –

(She pauses. An idea: start with a positive.)

Oh…My! Look at all those quiches, Dale.

DALE. I got all of the fluffier quiches –

WREN. Dale…honey –

DALE. but I could still grab the cheesier ones.

WREN. Dale –

DALE. Let me in, I might be able to get the others –

WREN. Dale…I can't. I can't…

(She tries to compose herself.)

There's been a…problem.

DALE. What do you mean?

WREN. Honey. We can't open the doors. They're permanently sealed shut.

*(**DALE** runs and tries to open the door. Wren screams and sobs. Dale walks back to the window. Defeated.)*

WREN. Oh, Dale. I'm so sorry. I wish it was me.

*(**DALE** nods. She puts her hand up to the glass. The ladies gasp. **WREN** puts her hand up on the glass. The others slowly join them – holding hands all together one last time.)*

(a moment)

*(**DALE** begins to sing slowly:)*

DALE.

WE ARE THE SUSAN B. ANTHONY...

ALL.

SOCIETY.
FOR THE SISTERS OF GERTRUDE STEIN.
WE ARE A STRONG AND VI-BA-RENT SOCIETY
TOGETHER TIL THE END OF ALL TIME
AND YOU KNOW WE STAND AS ONE,
OH MY, IS THAT QUICHE DONE?

*(A humongous, loud, terrifying splat. **DALE** explodes from the radiation. Leaving nothing but splatter on the window. The women scream in horror. They scream in horror some more. And then some more.)*

*(**LULIE** recovers the room by pulling **WREN**'s attention away from the splattered window.)*

LULIE. Wren, dear. She's gone.

*(**WREN** doesn't answer. **LULIE** stands in front of **WREN**. She looks her deep in the eyes. She takes her face in her hands.)*

LULIE. *(gently)* Wren. I know, honey. We all loved her very much. And we have so many wonderful memories of her to take with us. And I really, deeply in my heart,

have to think that there is no other way Dale would have wanted to go out:
Holding some of the finest quiches to grace God's holy earth. And for that, she is a saint in this new world. A world her little brother can help rebuild thanks to her sacrifice. A future, founded on the principles of Susan B. Anthony. Gertrude Stein. And Dale. Prist. She left so much of herself behind.

GINNY. *(Suddenly remembering!)* The quiches!

LULIE. Vern, let's get those in the freezer immediately.

VERN. On it.

*(**VERN** exits with the quiches.)*

LULIE. *(to **WREN**)* You see dear? Dale sacrificed herself so that her little brother could have EGG.

GINNY. It's true. He will survive now.

LULIE. The world will survive now. And the egg will carry on.

WREN. Yes. The egg.

*(**VERN** re-enters carrying a large portrait.)*

VERN. Hey, look what I found back there.

WREN. What is it?

VERN. Looks like the other portrait Dale had brought for us.

GINNY. The surprise!

WREN. *(she remembers)* Her new photo! Dale's photo! I want to see it!

*(**LULIE** reaches out and holds **WREN**'s hand.)*

VERN. It is with pride that I present to all of you, the legacy of our noble Saint Dale.

*(The emergency lights come up again. The sisters squint as **VERN** unveils the portrait. It is a portrait of two hands holding a single, beautiful egg. **DALE**'s charm dangles from the bracelet that matches **WREN**'s. The sisters are overcome.)*

LULIE. Oh, Wren...with all due respect to Lady Monmont, THAT is the most beautiful thing I've ever seen.

GINNY. Can we really survive four years down here?

VERN. Of course we can.

LULIE. We've got each other, don't we?

(The women all hold hands.)

(She sings:)

LULIE.

LINKED AS ONE.

ALL.

(LINKED AS ONE)

GINNY.

HAND IN HAND

ALL.

(HAND IN HAND)

WREN.

WE ARE STRONGER

ALL.

(WE ARE STRONGER)

VERN.

THAN ANY MAN!

(beat)

ALL.

WE ARE ONCE! TWICE! THREE TIMES A LADY!

WREN.

DALE SURE WAS A LADY –

(The lesbians take one last look at the splattered window.)

VERN. Damn straight she was!

LULIE. Amen!

ALL.

WHEN WE STAND TOGETHER AS

(The lesbians gather at **DALE***'s portrait.)*

ONE

(blackout)

APPENDIX

SCENE 3 LINE OPTIONS: EXAMPLES OF WHY AUDIENCE MEMBERS ARE LESBIANS

Below are some of the improvised lines from the original Off-Broadway run. Feel free to use any of these during Scene 3, or to make up your own! When the actors are improvising their own reasons why an audience member is a lesbian – it is important to use examples from their alternate universe rather than relying on stereotypes from our own. The more non sequitur the example – the more we found our audiences loved it.

- She knows all the differences between alligators and crocodiles! Who knows that?!
- She gives everyone little nicknames based on the drinks they drink or the hats they wear!
- She whittles her own toothpicks! And uses them!
- When she answers the phone, she says "Yellow?!"
- When we go out to dinner she uses the same fork for all six courses!
- She serves salad with a trowel and spade!
- She has 15 pairs of boots but last time I checked, she was not a cowboy!
- She pronounces app-ricot…APE-ricot!
- She buys five lipstick shades a month, but they're not for her. They're for her parakeet!
- I took a peek in her sewing kit and she's got a HACKSAW IN THERE.
- When she plants flowers in her yard, she practices shot put with the garden gnomes!
- She puts doilies on her doilies!
- I've seen her driving! Unaccompanied! To play golf!
- When she sketches nudes, she always leaves the socks on!
- She has a thimble collection and serves tea out of them!
- She breeds turtles!
- She thinks Mascara is a country in Africa!
- She keeps jars of saw dust around her house like potpourri!

- She doesn't go to the doctor. She just eats a clove of garlic and calls it a day!
- She uses her hair nets for catching fish in the stream!
- She makes lemonade without sugar.
- She dunks pumpernickel bread in her coffee!
- She uses all her kitchen utensils as jewelry!
- She owns three banjos!
- She can name all the bones in the foot.